THIS WALKER BOOK BELONGS TO:

_____

_____

_____

For Noah

First published 2005 by Walker Books Ltd, 87 Vauxhall Walk, London SE11 5HJ

This edition published 2006

12 14 16 18 20 19 17 15 13 11

© 2005 Jez Alborough

The right of Jez Alborough to be identified as author/illustrator of this work
has been asserted by him in accordance with the Copyright, Designs and Patents Act 1988

This book has been handlettered by Jez Alborough

Printed in China

British Library Cataloguing in Publication Data:
a catalogue record for this book is available from the British Library

ISBN 978-1-4063-0173-1

www.walker.co.uk

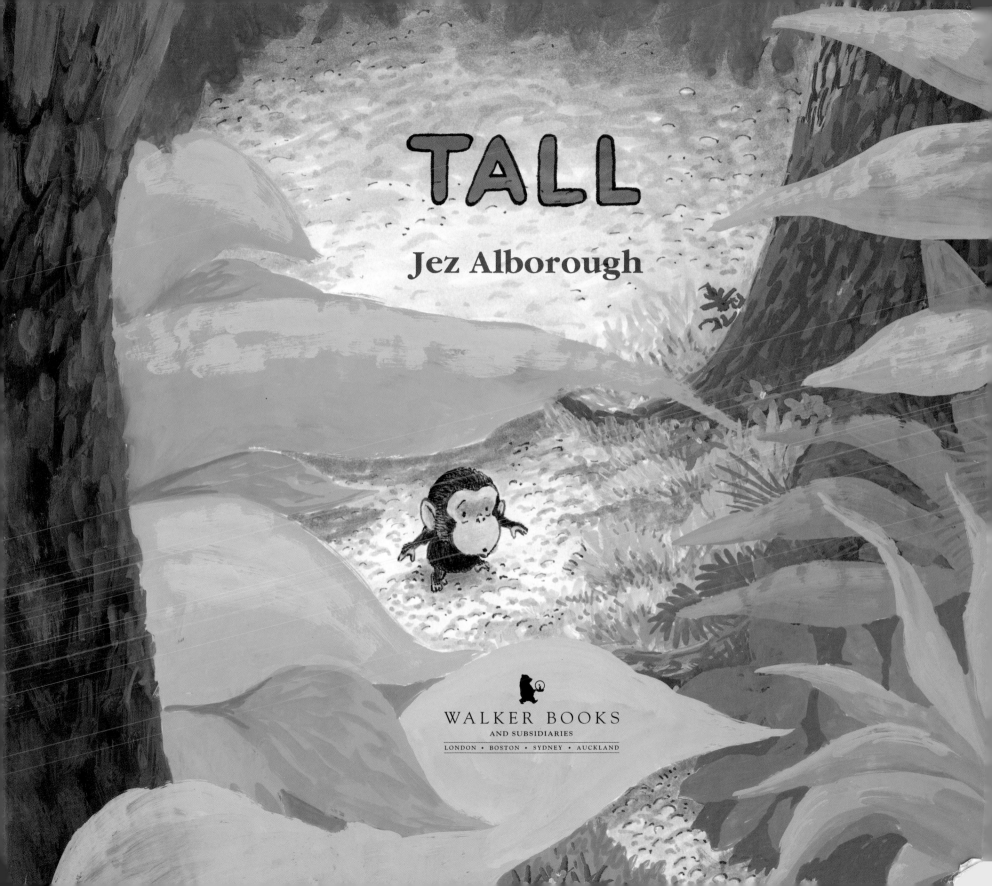

TALL

Jez Alborough

WALKER BOOKS
AND SUBSIDIARIES
LONDON · BOSTON · SYDNEY · AUCKLAND

Bobo – the little chimp in the jungle

ISBN: 978-0-7445-8273-4

ISBN: 978-1-4063-0173-1

ISBN: 978-1-4063-0456-5

Hug

All the animals in the jungle have someone to hug – except one little chimp. Will he ever get the hug he needs?

" The big, bright pictures dance off the page with such exuberance that you can't help but feel happy while you are looking at it." **Guardian**

Tall

Everyone seems to be taller than Bobo. But his friends help him to see that the size you are is the size you're meant to be!

Yes

At Bobo's bath time the little chimp shouts "YES". But at bedtime he cries "NO". It takes two friends and a lot of splashing to turn his "NO" into a "YES".